PooP
or Get Off the
POTTY!

Margaret McNamara

illustrated by
Allison Black

Henry Holt and Company
New York

Henry Holt and Company, *Publishers since 1866*
Henry Holt® is a registered trademark of Macmillan Publishing Group, LLC
175 Fifth Avenue, New York, NY 10010 • mackids.com

ISBN 978-1-250-12440-1
Library of Congress Control Number 2018945029

Our books may be purchased in bulk for promotional, educational, or business use. Please
contact your local bookseller or the Macmillan Corporate and Premium Sales Department at
(800) 221-7945 ext. 5442 or by e-mail at MacmillanSpecialMarkets@macmillan.com.

First edition, 2019 / Designed by Rebecca Syracuse
The art for this book was created digitally.
Printed in China by RR Donnelley Asia Printing Solutions Ltd.,
Dongguan City, Guangdong Province

1 3 5 7 9 10 8 6 4 2

For everyone who poops
—M. M.

To Zeppelin and Zoey,
our super pooper puppy duo
—A. B.

MIA

MASON

When Mason and Mia were babies,

they pooped a lot.

They even pooped double poops.

They pooped every different
kind of poop. All. The. Time.

Now Mason and Mia are ready.
Mason has a potty just for Mason.

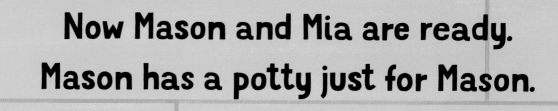

My potty,

he says.

MASON

Mia has a potty just for Mia.

My potty, she says.

Is the potty for naps?

says Mia.

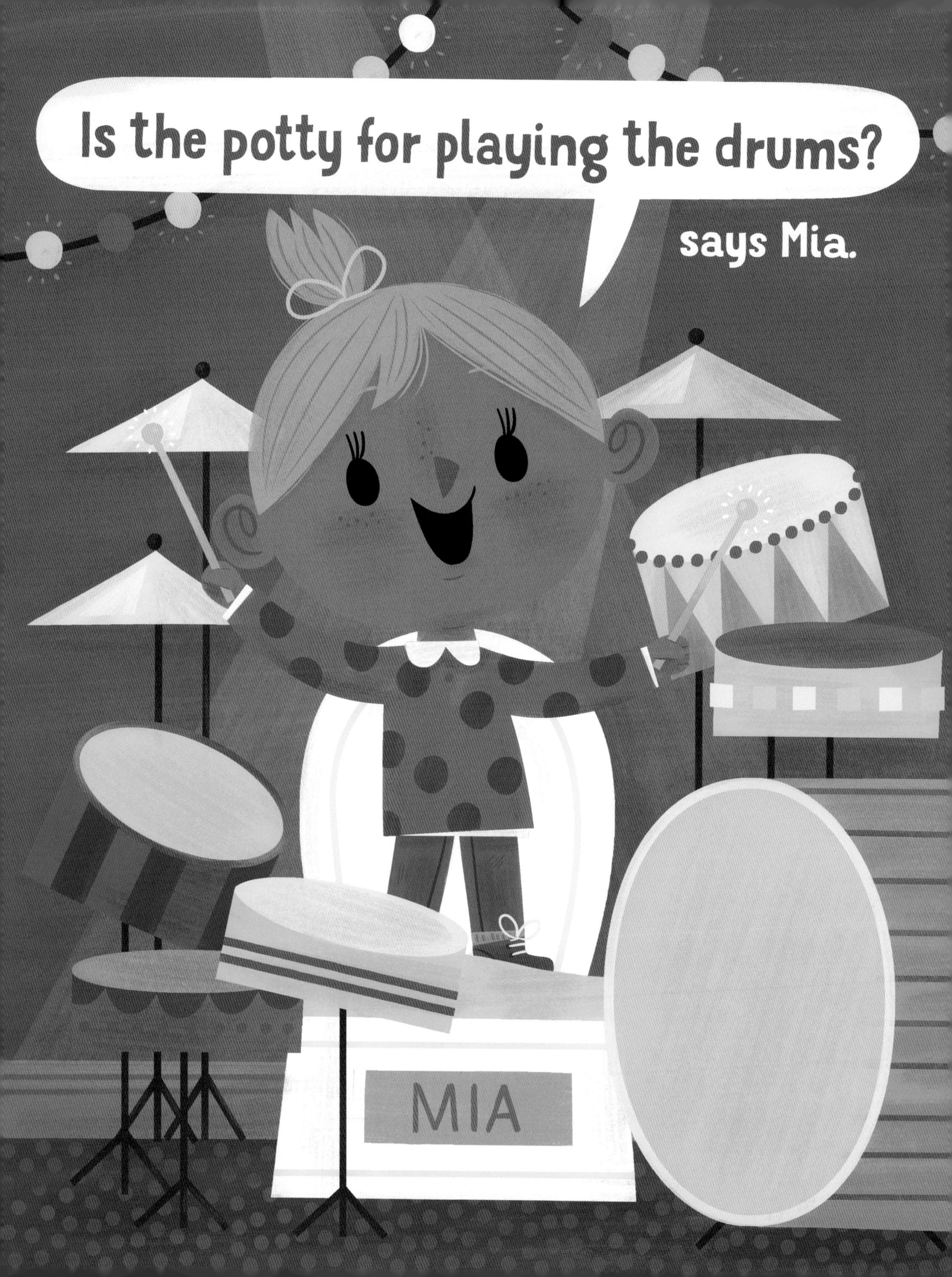
Is the potty for playing the drums?
says Mia.
MIA

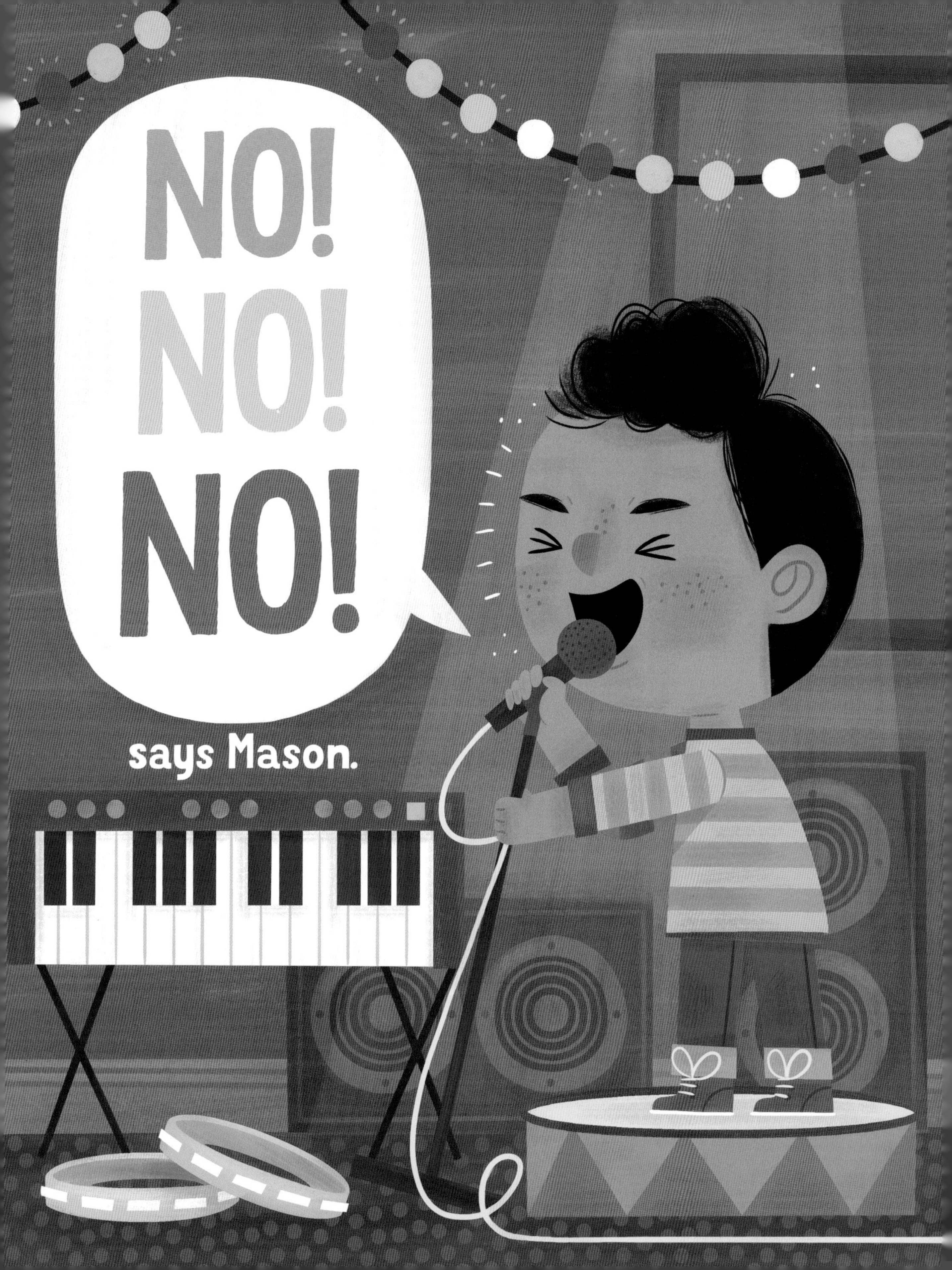

NO!
NO!
NO!

says Mason.

Now Mia isn't sure a poop is coming.
She waits for a minute.

Now Mason isn't sure a poop is coming.
He waits too.

Poop or get off the potty, Mia,

whispers Mason.

Mia's poop lands
RIGHT IN THE POTTY.

Mason's poop lands
RIGHT IN THE POTTY.

Time to
wipe!

I am a big kid now,

says Mia.

And they really are.